小红鸡和她的榖麦

The Little Red Hen and the Grains of Wheat

L. R. Hen

Jago

Touch the arrow with the RecorderPEN to start

Start   Info   English   Language

小红鸡和她的穀麦

The Little Red Hen and the Grains of Wheat

Retold by L.R.Hen

Illustrated by Jago

Mandarin translation by Sylvia Denham

Mantra Lingua

有一天，小红鸡走过农场庭院时看到一些穀麦。
「我可以种植这些小麦啊，」她想，「但是我会需要别人帮我。」

One day Little Red Hen was walking across the farmyard when she found some grains of wheat.
"I can plant this wheat," she thought. "But I'm going to need some help."

小红鸡向农场内其他的动物叫道：
「有谁会来帮我种植这些小麦啊？」
「我不能，」猫儿说，「我太忙了。」
「我不能，」小狗说，「我太忙了。」
「我不能，」鹅说，「我太忙了。」

Little Red Hen called out to the other animals on the farm:
"Will anyone help me plant this wheat?"
"Not I," said the cat, "I'm too busy."
"Not I," said the dog, "I'm too busy."
"Not I," said the goose, "I'm too busy."

「那么我便自己一个去做吧，」小红鸡说，
于是她便将谷麦拿去种植了。

"Then I shall do it all by myself," said Little Red Hen.
She took the grains of wheat and planted them.

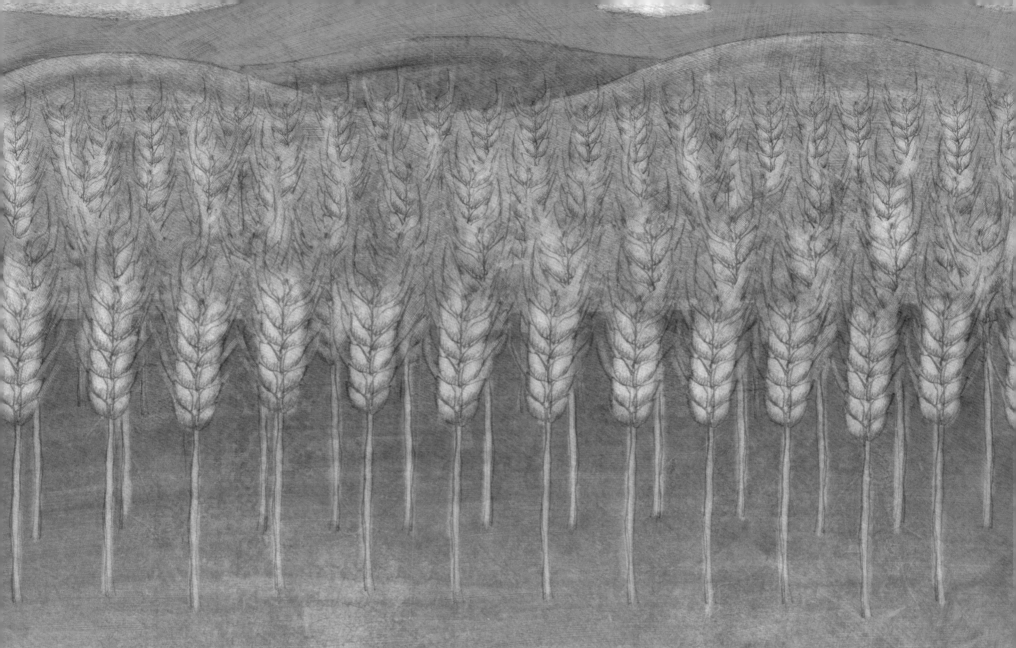

密云下雨，太阳照晒，小麦成长起来，又强壮，又高大，更是金黄色的。
有一天，小红鸡看到小麦长得成熟了，知道现在便是收割的时候了。

The clouds rained and the sun shone. The wheat grew strong and tall and golden.
One day Little Red Hen saw that the wheat was ripe. Now it was ready to cut.

小红鸡向其他的动物叫道：
「有谁会来帮我收割小麦啊？」
「我不能，」猫儿说，「我太忙了。」
「我不能，」小狗说，「我太忙了。」
「我不能，」鹅说，「我太忙了。」

Little Red Hen called out to the other animals:
"Will anyone help me cut the wheat?"
"Not I," said the cat, "I'm too busy."
"Not I," said the dog, "I'm too busy."
"Not I," said the goose, "I'm too busy."

「那么我便自己一个去做吧，」小红鸡说，
于是她便拿起镰刀将所有得小麦都割下来，然后将它们扎成一捆。

"Then I shall do it all by myself," said Little Red Hen.
She took a sickle and cut down all the wheat. Then she tied it into a bundle.

现在可以将小麦打穀脱粒了，
小红鸡把那捆小麦搬回农场的庭院去。

Now the wheat was ready to thresh.
Little Red Hen carried the bundle of wheat back to the farmyard.

小红鸡向其他的动物叫道：
「有谁会来帮将小麦打穀脱粒啊？」
「我不能，」猫儿说，「我太忙了。」
「我不能，」小狗说，「我太忙了。」
「我不能，」鹅说，「我太忙了。」

Little Red Hen called out to the other animals:
"Will anyone help me thresh the wheat?"
"Not I," said the cat, "I'm too busy."
"Not I," said the dog, "I'm too busy."
"Not I," said the goose, "I'm too busy."

「那么我便自己一个去做吧，」
小红鸡说。

"Then I shall do it all by myself!"
said Little Red Hen.

她花了一整天将小麦打穀脱粒，
当她做完之后，
她便把穀麦搬到她的拖拉车去。

She threshed the wheat all day long.
When she had finished she put it into her cart.

现在可以将小麦拿去磨成面粉了，但是小红鸡觉得很疲倦，于是她便走进榖仓，她很快便睡着了。

Now the wheat was ready to grind into flour. But Little Red Hen was very tired so she went to the barn where she soon fell fast asleep.

第二天早上，小红鸡向其他的动物叫道：
「有谁会来帮我将小麦拿到磨坊去啊？」
「我不能，」猫儿说，「我太忙了。」
「我不能，」小狗说，「我太忙了。」
「我不能，」鹅说，「我太忙了。」

The next morning Little Red Hen called out to the other animals:
"Will anyone help me take the wheat to the mill?"
"Not I," said the cat, "I'm too busy."
"Not I," said the dog, "I'm too busy."
"Not I," said the goose, "I'm too busy."

「那么我便自己一个去吧，」小红鸡说，
于是她便拖著她那满载穀麦的拖拉车，一直拉到磨坊去。

"Then I shall go all by myself!" said Little Red Hen.
She pulled her cart full of wheat and wheeled it all the way to the mill.

磨坊主取过小麦，将它们辗磨成面粉，
现在可以用它来造面包了。

The miller took the wheat and ground it into flour.
Now it was ready to make a loaf of bread.

小红鸡向其他的动物叫道：

「有谁会来帮我将面粉拿到面包师傅处啊？」

「我不能，」猫儿说，「我太忙了。」

「我不能，」小狗说，「我太忙了。」

「我不能，」鹅说，「我太忙了。」

Little Red Hen called out to the other animals:

"Will anyone help me take this flour to the baker?"

"Not I," said the cat, "I'm too busy."

"Not I," said the dog, "I'm too busy."

"Not I," said the goose, "I'm too busy."

「那么我便自己一个去吧，」小红鸡说，
于是她便把那袋面粉一直拿到面包店去。

"Then I shall go all by myself!" said Little Red Hen.
She took the heavy sack of flour all the way to the bakery.

面包师傅取过面粉，加入酵母、水、糖和盐，
他跟着把生面团放入烤炉烘烤。
当面包烤完后，他便把面包交给小红鸡。

The baker took the flour and added some yeast, water, sugar and salt.
He put the dough in the oven and baked it.
When the bread was ready he gave it to Little Red Hen.

小红鸡拿着新鲜烤好的面包一
直走回农场的庭院。

Little Red Hen carried the freshly baked bread
all the way back to the farmyard.

小红鸡向其他的动物叫道：
「有谁会来帮我吃这个新鲜美味的面包啊？」

Little Red Hen called out to the other animals:
"Will anyone help me eat this tasty fresh bread?"

「我会，」小狗说，「我有空啊。」

"I will," said the dog, "I'm not busy."

「我会，」鹅说，「我有空啊。」

"I will," said the goose, "I'm not busy."

「我会，」猫儿说，「我有空啊。」

"I will," said the cat, "I'm not busy."

「啊！让我先考虑一下！」小红鸡说。

"Oh, I'll have to think about that!"
said Little Red Hen.

小红鸡邀请了磨坊主和面包师傅来分享她那美味可口的面包，而其他三只动物只能在旁观看。

The Little Red Hen invited the miller and the baker to share her delicious bread while the three other animals all looked on.

key words

little	小	clouds	云
red	红	rain	雨
hen	鸡	sun	太阳
farmyard	农场庭院	ripe	成熟
farm	农场	plant	种植
goose	鹅	cut	收割
dog	狗	sickle	镰刀
cat	猫	bundle	捆
wheat	小麦	thresh	打穀
busy	忙	grind	辗磨

主要的生字

flour	面粉	tasty	美味
the mill	磨坊	fresh	新鲜
miller	磨坊主	delicious	可口
ground	辗磨	all	所有
bread	面包	she	她
baker	面包师傅	he	他
yeast	酵母		
water	水		
sugar	糖		
salt	盐		

First published in 2005 by Mantra Lingua

Global House, 303 Ballards Lane London N12 8NP
www.mantralingua.com
Text copyright © 2005 Henriette Barkow
Illustration copyright © 2005 Jago
Dual language text copyright © Mantra Lingua
Audio copyright © 2008 Mantra Lingua
This sound enabled edition published 2012

A CIP record of this book is available from the British Library

Printed in Hatfield,UK FP050712PB08122126

Little Red Hen finds some grains of wheat but when she asks
the cat, the dog and the goose to help her plant them, they are all too busy!

Enjoy a unique interactive experience with TalkingPEN books. Listen to familiar stories come alive with words, sounds and music. You and your children can record yourselves, then save and playback page by page with TalkingPEN. Ideal for developing language skills - listening, reading and creative storytelling.

The Little Red Hen is available in 37 dual language editions: English with Albanian, Arabic, Bengali, Bulgarian, Chinese (Cantonese), Croatian, Farsi, French, German, Greek, Gujarati, Hindi, Hungarian, Italian, Japanese, Korean, Kurdish, Latvian, Lithuanian, Norwegian, Panjabi, Polish, Portuguese, Romanian, Russian, Shona, Simplified Chinese (Mandarin), Somali, Spanish, Swahili, Swedish, Tagalog, Tamil, Turkish, Urdu, Vietnamese or Yoruba. An English Only edition is also available. For information about the TalkingPEN, demonstration videos, and a list of audio files for this book, please visit www.mantralingua.com.

Winner of the
National Literacy Association
WOW! Award 2006

MANTRA LINGUA
connecting communities

MANDARIN & ENGLISH
ISBN 978-1-84611-212-6

9 781846 112126 >